T0199193

Drowning in Metaphors

illuminating your
honey cream color,
My eyes
deeply search

Mystic somber
it knows to survive

a jaded ghost
lingering in the shadows

it ruptured my sanity

in search
for peace

going to ascend

empty promise

lustrous lips
grip my cheeks

live in a fantasy

looking
into my own
reflection

my eyes
gaze upon
its wonder

cool breeze
gently blowing
lies within your beauty
I am now their voice
spontaneous
combustion
imprinted on a leaf

each their
own person

gently
graced

FATIMA SALAHUDDIN

AuthorHouse™
1663 Liberty Drive
Bloomington, IN 47403
www.authorhouse.com
Phone: 1 (800) 839-8640

This book is printed on acid-free paper.

ISBN: 978-1-7283-2569-9 (sc)
ISBN: 978-1-7283-2570-5 (e)

Library of Congress Control Number: 2019913154

Print information available on the last page.

Published by AuthorHouse 09/04/2019

authorHOUSE®

Drowning in Metaphors

F ATIMA S ALAHUDDIN

Acknowledgement

I WOULD LIKE TO give recognition to the creator who is responsible for everything that exist and beyond. I am honored for what the creator has given me even waking up to another morning. All my success and failures cannot be possible without the creator's blessing, so I am grateful to be given an opportunity to live and learn from both my successes and my failures. The gift of support and encouragement that I received from my family and professors who never shied away from giving their honest opinions and critiques to try and do better, to be better has help me tremendously. Especially, when it came to my writing, there were many times when I got my feelings hurt by people's honest criticism however, I knew that if I wanted to be a better writer then I had no choice, but to put my feelings aside. So thank you, to all my English professors who saw potential and didn't give up on me, thank you to my family who always pushed me outside of my comfort zone in order to be a better me and a special thank you to my father, my greatest support system of all, thank you for everything.

Beauty

Fatima Salahuddin

WHERE ARE YOU *from?* You with black, bold curls illuminating your honey cream color which defines your exterior. My eyes deeply search for the ones we no longer recognize. The ones we long to remember. I ask *where are you from?* Where did your name Zainab come from? Where does your strange clothing from head to toe come from? Why do I find your existence strange yet familiar? Your smooth, sable color gracing every inch of your skin. The tranquil warmth exuding from your ebony eyes draws me closer to what feels like home. Tell me, *where are you from?*

You, who utters words like كيف **حالك**, انشالله, الحمد لله, - a part of me yearns to understand them. To embrace them. To accept this puzzle piece in hopes it will unlock gates to my forgotten home. You, who wears the sun's rays upon your head like a crown, as I stand from the outside looking into my own reflection, hoping and praying you will see me as your brother, your sister. I want you to teach me what I have lost and forgotten. Will you welcome me back home in your strong embrace? Will your full, lustrous lips grip my cheeks? Will you tell me *where you are from?*

Where is the labyrinth giving way to precious gems scattered around like fine dunes across the Saharan Desert? Like the mountains sitting on both sides of the valley tall and high. With its presence commanding silence as my eyes gaze upon its wonder. I ask, *where are you from?* Where can I find home again? As I stand in the moonlit desert with a cool breeze gently blowing sand across my feet. I look upon rows filled with my ancestors looking back at me. Telling me life is merely a journey in order to find home in the next, but all of what triggers my memory from our past lives lies within your beauty.

Shattered Hearts

knew the day would come,
When the sun would shine upon your face.
When you would stop the flow of everything,
Stripping the life of Neptune from down below.
The day you would become consumed by the unknown world,
I knew then, I would no longer see your glowing red hair.

I tried to keep my angel with her beautiful red hair,
But I knew the day would come,
When she began collecting things from the unknown world.
When the sun no longer shines upon her face.
When our creator no longer grace us down below,
As her presence began to change everything.

Indeed, her presence changed everything,
When his indigo eyes tainted her luscious red hair.
When the opulence of his essence lured her from below,
I saw and knew the day would come.
I couldn't keep the darkness from consuming her face,
As she left the only place she's known, her world.

When you ascended above it shattered my world,
And along with it everything.
Now here we are face to face,
As I can no longer see your red hair.
I knew the day would come,
When my people marched alongside me and emerged from below.

Indeed, we emerged from down below,

And into the unknown world.

I knew the day would come,

When the pain you suffered would devour everything.

The darkness within bled into your eyes and soiled your red hair,

From the one who swore his love to you, but instead brought tears to your face.

When I look at your face,

I do not see the girl who brought me happiness down below.

Or the girl that had glowing red hair,

And always breathed life into my world.

All I see is a monster that stole everything,

But how can I complain when I knew this day would come.

I tried to shield her from this world, even though I knew this day would come.

The day when black lays to rest on her hair and the day I will no longer see her face.

Because today I lost everything especially my little girl from down below.

Zahra

ntranced by endless depths of blue.
Sometimes I hear your cry down below,
Where you became captured by its loom.

Knowing your elsewhere, taunts me into gloom.
Remembering your sweet sound seemed long ago.
Entranced by endless depths of blue.

It is hard to embrace your hue,
When it swept you into the unknown,
Where you became captured by its loom.

I cry to the brightly lit moon,
Surrendering all of me in pure snow.
Entranced by endless depths of blue.

They intertwine and burst from my view.
From afar I can hear its bellow,
Where you became captured by its loom.

I remember how the waves once soothed you,
Completely tranquil and serene as you glowed.
Entranced by endless depths of blue.
Where you became captured by its loom.

Evil

Inside

An infinite fall, in a bottomless pit of emptiness should have been my grave. There is no mercy for the beast who ravaged them all

As their corpses lay to waste.

Such poor souls, they never saw the beast coming as it disguised itself.

They believed that their own could do no harm against them, but they were wrong.

Their naiveness left them vulnerable to deceit

And the door to their flesh and bones open for the taking.

How can a beast such as this resist the raging hunger from within?

A beast who feels nothing when its blades of fury penetrate defenseless souls; When it sends the flames of hell to rain down on them with tyranny;

When the cries for mercy fall on def ears and cold hearts.

Tell me, how can I not succumb to the darkness that weakens mortals?

The opportunity is as sweet as honey from its nectar.

After all, I am the beast that wages wars, turns brother against brother, corrupts all that is good and destroys unity amongst the people.

I am the evil that should be imprisoned and kept away from the hands of humanity, Yet here I stand as the imposter;

Pretending to be the sword of justice for the powerless,

And the protector for the defenseless.

I stand as the sovereign ruler over the hearts of Man, a beast who reigns supreme.

Naseeb

(THE ONE)

You embraced me into your world
And greeted me with a smile
Only given to those worthy.
I lived a great portion of my youth,
But was never fully satisfied until you
Found your way to me.

When your eyes laid upon
Every inch of my flesh,
Before any words escaped
From our lips;
You knew, you felt, you believed
That this fading light was your Naseeb.

Submerged in solitude, I look at my reflection
As I struggle to see a queen that you saw in me.
Tears flowed from my eyes like a stream,
Pulled by the force of my emotions,
Buried from within as they slowly reached the surface.

My reflection was of a young lady
Who never felt deserving of love, attention, or affection.
That trip I made across the world changed my life.
That unexpected encounter locked and intertwined our eyes.
Though the encounter was short lived,
The feeling between us was forever.
Since that moment, I knew, I felt, I believed

His handsome smile, with eyes that didn't shy away from
Looking beyond my flesh, but into my soul.
I reflect on the years of my youth
As I continued living with a seal on my eyes.
Not being able to see a glimpse of the woman I am today.

Wasting my life away in misery
And not even knowing you were coming.
That this entire time you were sent to come for me,
To head in my direction.
To embrace me with your love and affection,
Beyond my youth as I am now old and grey.

Till this day, I still don't feel deserving of you
I guess that's just me, but when I look into
My reflection I begin to see that queen you saw in me.
No words can express how grateful I am that you knew,
You felt and you believed in me to be your Naseeb.

Black Rose

EYES ADORNED IN pure, majestic, azure gazed down at the repulsive color of my petals. The opulence of blooming, scarlets, that brightly, lit, the garden surrounding a chivalrous man did not sway his benevolent eyes from me. The roses were graced with divine beauty. I was not granted to share the same fate as they. Though I could not see the beauty in which your benevolent eyes sought out within me, I continued to fall to the spark you ignited within the most hardened part of myself.

Eyes adorned in pure, majestic, azure lit a flame to a heart covered in the frigid grips of darkness. Each passing day, you devoted your time to a rose unworthy of every facet of your entirety. I remember feeling honored by your words, which I held on to for as long as I could. Each day when you were in my presence it felt like an opening to a new beginning.

Eyes once adorned in pure, majestic, azure slowly succumbed to their own vice. A rose outcast from its own kind, stripped of its beauty from the tips of its petals down to the end of its stem. A rose to be forever cursed in darkness, suddenly emerged into light and transformed in absolute splendor.

Every scarlet rose once envied by their repulsive sister now looks upon her illuminating umber skin in admiration. Her hair that harmoniously flows like the swaying of the ocean's tides and gently unravels in an endless spiral of black wonder, crowning her head in majesty. No longer a rose covered in black and entranced by the whispers of darkness, she now rises amongst her own as their queen.

The Garden Queen gazing at the moon softly hummed sweet sounds of melodies. She continued to let them flow from between her lips until she heard sounds from a familiar voice. A voice she knew and was eager to reunite with once again, a voice she would soon learn was not from the gentlemen she perceived him to be. The Garden Queen left the confines of her palace in hopes of reuniting with the one who gave his blood and pledged himself to her for eternity.

She arrived at his palace and entered the massive ballroom submerged in an array of luxuriant attire worn by the most prominent guests. They rhythmically swayed to their hearts content with their faces jeweled in exotic veils, disguising them in grandeur. However, the queen saw beyond their veils and began to grow greatly concerned for the prince. All she could see in their eyes was their lust for his wealth and power. As they gave their dubious smiles and hollow words of "kindness" to the prince, the Garden Queen became saddened for she could no longer hear his heart that once strongly beat the radiance of life. His heart as black as the night's sky and hard as stone bled its poison straight into his soul. As she stood from afar completely lost in confusion and pain, her eyes looked deeply into his. His eyes were malevolent which shattered her heart into pieces. The prince remained at his throne, as he continued to stare down at the Garden Queen's umber skin when suddenly a beggar found his way into the ball.

The beggar came up to the prince and pleaded with him, in hopes that he would spread a small portion of his wealth to feed the poor. The prince summoned one of his servants that held a tray mounted with roasted fowl; he grabbed a piece from it as he looked down at the beggar. He then arrogantly uttered to all whom lent their ears "I am divinity in the flesh, I have ascended from amongst you, I am now a supreme deity; worship and devote your lives to me and you shall be rewarded."

The pompous prince continued with his rhetoric as he bit into the meat from the piece of fowl in his hand and chewed it endlessly. He placed the piece of fowl back on the tray held by his servant as he stepped down from his throne and stood in front of the beggar. With his mouth full of mush from the persistent chewing, he slowly drooled the mush onto the ballroom floor and commanded the beggar to feast upon his generosity.

There was not a sound as the beggar struggled to adhere to his majesty's command. The beggar began to whimper as he slowly kneeled on one knee after another until, he found himself on all fours hovered over the mush. Then suddenly, the queen's voice soared throughout the monstrosity of the ballroom directly towards the prince. "Your eyes are no longer adorned in pure, majestic, azure; no longer do they stand for hope and prosperity. You were never superior from those amongst you, nor will you ever be."

The prince, infuriated by her words, ordered his guards to cast the Garden Queen out from his site. "You are consumed by the vice buried inside you. The light of hope will never reach your heart, for your fate is sealed." But before the guards could reach the Garden Queen, the doors slammed shut to her command leaving no way out to escape. Every living soul instantly panicked in horror, as they began to lose their sense of civility and spiraled into the depths of madness. They all ravaged each other's flesh, leaving their blood smeared everywhere. Their corpses laid torn apart and scattered across the floor, with not one single soul left breathing except for the beggar and the prince. The queen moved towards the cowardly, frightened prince as the ends of her dress were drug through the blood of the dead. She stood at a distance from him as he cried and begged for mercy. "You gave your blood to me, you pledged yourself to me! And still you betrayed your pledge to me!!"

As tears surfaced from the eyes of the Garden Queen, she began to chant a curse upon the Prince.

"Your Royal Palace is now your eternal dwelling place in hell. Be the hideous beast that you are from within your heart." The queen immediately turned her back, as the beast from within the Prince started taking form. While she began to leave the cursed Palace, the beast relentlessly begged for her mercy. But it was too late, for the queen had seen the true essence of his heart. He tried to run after her, but the curse hindered him. It began to sear his skin black and crush every bone in his body. The Garden Queen approached the frightened beggar with an enchanting scarlet rose, she looked down upon him and said: "A tale as old as time, will spread across lands like fire as the sun will rise to usher in a new age. A tale of a chivalrous man once adorned with eyes of hope and prosperity for the future, became the horrid beast instead. Come with me to a place unknown to Man, a place of eternal youth and serenity, a place where you will suffer no more." And so, the beggar took hold of the queen's hand and into the unknown never to be seen again.

The Guardian

*I*T HAS BEEN so long, since the last time I inhaled you into the core depths of me. Since the last time, I gazed upon your mystic somber infecting all of London as you created a squalid, wretched, side to a place I once called home. The memories of my god forsaken homeland consumed by lust, greed, hierarchy, and exploitation. My home, a cursed tomb for the gutted, slashed, and ripped people of the impoverished land washed up on the shores of London. My home always thirsts for blood, it's the only way it knows to survive; It is the infamous London killer, victimizing its prey yet it portrays itself as the merciful guardian of light watching over its people.

Indeed, the Cathedrals in our city which only emits undeniable grace and beauty observes everything in light and in darkness. However, the grace and beauty from our beloved edifice (St. Paul) had a faint presence amongst its people. It lacked striking that fear of the God Almighty, into the hearts of many tainted by their own as well as society's impure desires. I was once a driven young lady inspired by the words of God or so I thought; it wasn't until my father a former surgeon at the Royal Hospital in Whitechapel on the East End of London.

It wasn't until then, when my father unlike many decided to educate me on what he loved most. I always stood beside him in front of his subject's deathly, cold, corpse that laid on his steel worktable.

I felt completely honored, to be my father's student in a line of work tailored only for men. Although I was never taught how to perform surgery in a proper setting like a university or college, I still could not hold back the feeling of excitement when the sharp, non-serrated, blade of my scalpel cut into the flesh so smoothly. That day was special, it was the day that I proved to my father of my potential worth to medicine. It was the day that I laid a perfectly clean incision on the dead body, it was the day I realized in that moment I had become something more.

Mother was perfect and angelic, she supported me in my wild endeavor of becoming the first English woman surgeon in Whitechapel. When father called my ambition rubbish at the time, mother always stood firm encouraging me to be steadfast in making my dream, my ambition a reality. Mother was the strong knot that kept our family tied together, mother was everything I could never be. In late June she was finally laid to rest after suffering severely from an illness. An illness doctors as well as my father diagnosed as cancer, a disease that stripped away mother's long locks, depleted mother's body weight as her bones were frail like glass. Each passing day she neared closer to death until it finally consumed her last breath of life, now it was just father and me.

It has been a while, since the last time father spoke to me. The last time he taught me his craft as a surgeon. The last time we sat down together for supper, since mother's passing, he became more like a jaded ghost lingering in the shadows. What made him think he could just simply abandon everything he worked so hard to gain and maintain? How could he just give up on his life? How could he simply drown himself into the clutches of transgression? Did mother and I ever mean anything to him? Those questions forever taunted me adrift into the unknown misery that consumed me entirely. Then suddenly, I heard a voice of an angel a voice so comforting and perfect. That voice whispered a reposeful sound in my ear, it was a melody sung to me as a little girl growing up by my mother.

I was elated to see her once more, to feel her presence beside me however, our reunion was cut short. Mother had a purpose and I was her tool to fulfill it, so that her soul can finally rest in peace. She told me everything about father that I was too blind to see; mother believed that father was special and so did I, despite the fact that he allowed himself to become tainted by the infernal East End, consumed by the wicked harlots with their resonating voices of the blackened streets. Our desire to purify his body required removing the venom he grew an addiction towards; I wore my father's clothes and learned to imitate proper Englishmen gestures accustomed to the East End slums.

Inconspicuously, I followed my father into the darkness and watched him feast on the "alluring" night walker named Polly, that's what he called the repulsive crone right after he gave a piece of himself to her. Night walkers like her care for nothing except money, not only did she take my father's money, but she took a piece of my father with her. That burned my core, it shattered my heart, and it ruptured my sanity; after he left, I followed Polly a little ways down the street, then shortly after I struck her fiercely with the Might of God through my sharp, non-serrated, blade. I ripped away the harlot's resonating voice, enabling her to utter any shred of sound. I proceeded further with her body by disposing her entrails on Buck's Row where I left her deathly, corpse.

One by one, my blade ravaged their flesh and stole their souls. All five of those harlots I slaughtered were my father's favorite, Mary Ann Nichols (Polly), Annie Chapman, Elizabeth Stride, Catherine (Kate) Eddowes, and Mary Jeanette Kelly. I hope father will love them more dead than alive, as I made their flesh the main ingredient for supper. Tell me father, do they taste the same to you or better from when they were alive? Does their putrid skin melt in your mouth like butter on a warm piece of bread? I wanted to ask him those questions that were spinning in my head and hear his answers, instead I struck father in the back of his head which knocked him out cold. Father looked so peaceful in that chair, although he was tied to it firmly. For a moment I marveled at father and thought about all he has done for me and mother, how he made us into the strong women that we are. When mother passed away, she never truly left us, she was that merciful guardian of light watching over her family.

I slowly poured kerosene on father as he remained unconscious, and then I poured the rest on myself. I looked at him one last time and whispered, "we must purify ourselves from the toxins of this world, in order to join our beloved in the next." Soon after, father and I were disintegrated into dust by the power in which the flames possessed. We became unified with the earth as our purified souls drift into the unknown world in search for mother, the Guardian of Light.

I

And

The City

"*I*'M WRITING IN this book to anyone who still has a beating heart and a soul. I want to tell the world about my home that was taken from me and about my people that lost more than just their lives but lost their will to speak; I am now their voice."

Serenity that was the name of our home, it used to be a place where trees stood on opposing sides with their enormous height hovering the road that led to our gates. They almost appeared as if they were welcoming those into Serenity. It was a place where the rays from the sun rising, till the sun setting always gently graced our precious land. It truly was a serene place that exuded tranquility and equality. It was a trustworthy place where you could surrender the most vital parts of oneself, the heart and soul.

It is no longer that place, no longer does it hold that name. It hurts so much, to live what we have lived through since then and having to watch every aspect of our society change, was more than what we could bare. We are still enduring unimaginable things that you would only hear about happening elsewhere, but not here. Our home was a place where there were once good and wholesome people, each their own person, as free as a bird. They were honest people and we were once united like a family, sharing the same foundation of ethics as normalcy flourished through our beloved city.

Now 15 years later, our home is a place of lifeless people. A place where darkness is now our light and far removed from our destitute land, lie the ten districts known as The Elite, they are the primary cause of our disunity, dismay, and despair. Their tyrannical ways have permeated the hearts and minds of everyone, making them believe that the only one's worthy of living are The Elite. They have drained us of our resources, our waters, and minerals that once enriched the land. The affluence that once gave way to the technology that made this city and its people flow proficiently, like the undulate imprinted on a leaf is no longer to our advantage.

Sadly, many of us have forgotten who we once were; we don't even recognize our own reflection. Their ideology has done its job by stripping those memories away, leaving us vulnerable to their belief system that rapidly grew like a spontaneous combustion taking over. We live in ground zero, where the remains from our defeat lay in a pool of shattered hope that once lit a flame in our hearts. We believed that with our strong conviction in fighting against our enemy to prevent an invasion, that we would be the ones to prevail to victory.

The buildings, the roads, every home of all who once lived and died here all tell the story of that tragic day. Ground zero is a place that reflects the truth, but nobody wants to be exposed to the truth, most of us want to live in a fantasy. We have drastically gone from a people and to each their own identity, to now a broken community labeled as the unwanted. We have been forced to be the entertainment of The Elite. Once every year we are obligated to participate in an inhumane event which consist of a single terrifying rule; two members of each family are to battle one another to the death, and whosoever is left standing gets to ascend to one of the ten districts.

This barbaric practice is simultaneously a part of our existence. Many of us in ground zero take part in it religiously, we prepare for it, we sharpen and create effective weapons for it, and all of this is done for those who desire to feel belonged, to feel human once again. Even if that means becoming the very monster you loathe, becoming that soulless creature that can chain its rival to the back end of a pickup truck and drag him around in the arena like a rag doll. Or perhaps seeing them rip each other's heads off like plucking a grape from its vine.

I lost both brothers to this vicious cycle. One day I heard them both conversing over their plans in how one of them was going to ascend, as if it was an honor to sacrifice your own and to be sacrificed for the so called "greater good." It was then that I decided to leave from this poison, this illusion that we were uncivilized before they came along. As if we needed their existence to grace our land and bless our people with their brutality inflicted upon us.

I fear that we may never wake up long enough to break the cycle of this infectious illusion of needing them to legitimize who we are. They give their empty promise of freedom dangling it in our faces, as though we are a pack of hungry wolves. Maybe we are just a pack of hungry wolves desperately waiting for them to liberate us. After desecrating our homeland; they have molded us into the hungry wolves that we are. It is a cursed fate my people have and will continue to suffer from. So, I was confronted with two adverse decisions, it was either parting ways from this place and out into the desiccated lands left with nothing but a malnourished shell or die a brutal death.

Before I made it out of the confines of our city, I looked up at the enormous screen in the town's square televising the event with breaking news. It was reported to the public that, for the first time in the 15 years of its existence we have witnessed no ascension. I saw the faces of the two men that laid lifeless on the ground. I saw how they dragged those men, how they just left them there as the game proceeded on to their next contestants. I was left with nothing but only my tears whimpering beneath my breath "my brothers, they're gone." I resumed and continued to walk beyond the city's limits leaving behind the infinite illusion, disillusion, and the promise that was fed to us by The Elite in order to preserve their rule; I have embraced the ugly truth instead, in search for peace.

Printed in the United States
By Bookmasters